orson

orson

BY **Rascal**

●

ILLUSTRATED BY
Mario Ramos

LOTHROP, LEE & SHEPARD BOOKS · NEW YORK

Orson was a bear—the biggest and strongest in all the forest. From woodpecker to wolf, from robin to raccoon, everyone was afraid of him.

There wasn't an animal that didn't remember the time when Orson played blindman's buff and nearly squashed the hare and the tortoise, or the time he played leapfrog and broke the poor moose's antlers.

Ever since, Orson had been sad
and lonely. He was happy only
at the end of autumn, when he
knew that winter was coming
and he would soon be able
to hibernate and forget
everything.

Of course, in the spring he woke up again. To his despair, nothing had changed during his sleep. He was still more than six feet tall. He still outweighed every animal for miles around. And his cave was still as cramped and messy as ever. There was only one little thing that was different: A small bear was sitting under the big oak tree just outside his door.

"What are you doing in front of my door?" asked Orson.
"Haven't you heard about me? Go back where you came from.
I don't need anyone!" But from time to time, Orson poked his
head out of his cave. "Are you still there? Why aren't you afraid
of me? Are you deaf or stupid? Go on then, go away!"

When night fell, the little bear hadn't budged an inch. Puzzled, Orson picked him up. Right away he understood why this little bear was so brave, and his laughter rang through the forest. "You're a teddy bear, left behind and forgotten like me! But you're welcome here—we're from the same family, after all."

Orson made a little crib out of an old drawer. He was very happy not to be alone anymore. From now on, there would be someone to share his life with. That night, Orson dreamed he had a son.

The next morning, just for a second, he thought his dream had come true. "This is no place for a little bear," he said to himself. He tucked the teddy into the highest drawer and cleaned his house from top to bottom, and the whole time he was washing and scrubbing, he didn't once stop talking to his new friend. "Talking makes me feel so much better," he told him. "How I wish you could talk back. I would so much like to see you alive and smiling! It's hard to tell if you are happy or sad in your little stuffed heart."

The next day, the moose saw them swimming in the lake.

The day after that, the woodcock saw them fishing.

From then on, not a day passed without someone seeing them together: at the bend in a forest path, perched in a tall tree, stretched out on the green grass, or being chased by a swarm of bees. Who was Orson's mysterious companion? they all wondered. A cousin from Europe? A nephew? His son? No one knew, but everyone was sure of this: Orson had a friend and he looked very happy.

Still, when the trees turned red, the little bear was still just a stuffed toy. Orson had not been able to bring him to life. So when the day came to hibernate, he decided to put the teddy bear back where he'd found him nine months before. Hugging him one last time, he placed him at the foot of the big oak tree. What a sad and lonely winter this would be. With a lump in his throat, Orson headed into his cave.

He had scarcely taken three
steps inside his door when
a little voice called out to
him. It wouldn't be
a lonely winter
after all!